PICTURES BY Sam Usher

THE Secret RAILWAY
and the CRYSTAL CAVES

OXFORD
UNIVERSITY PRESS

TICKETS PLEASE!

WAIT! STOP RIGHT THERE!

SORRY! But you'll need a ticket before you go any further. And I'm not giving tickets out to just anyone, you know. Especially not if you're a spy for Griselda—the evil Clockmaker. What's that? You're a Warm Heart, 100% child, human? You're not a clockwork spy? Come off it. Who are you trying to fool, with your sharp tin fingers and your piercing metal eyes? Don't think you'll get past me that easily. If you've been spying on Ella and Leo, and are trying to stop them from defeating the evil Clockmaker and returning the stolen magical objects of Izzambard to their rightful owners, then you can think again. There is **NO WAY** that I'm letting you on board this journey.

Why are you sticking out your tongue? Oh. To prove you're a Warm Heart? No clockwork bits at all? Hmm. Well, OK. Though I'm going to need more proof than that. Griselda makes some amazing creations. But I've got my ways of finding out if you're a clockwork spy. You'll have to answer these foolproof questions. If your answers are **'YES'** then you're definitely clockwork and you may come **NO FURTHER!** But if your answers are **'NO'**, then you may collect your ticket and continue—full steam ahead—into a world of mystery, magic, and adventure.

Right. Are you ready? Then concentrate,
please:

QUESTION 1 Are you frightened of tin openers
and magnets?

QUESTION 2 Do you want to be a tractor
when you grow up?

QUESTION 3 Is engine oil your favourite drink?

QUESTION 4 Do you work for a terrifying
Clockmaker called Griselda?

QUESTION 5 Are you easy to wind up
. . . with a key?

Are all your answers 'NO?' Excellent. And thank goodness for that! You are **definitely not** a clockwork spy. Here's your ticket:

ALL ABOARD!
THE Secret
RAILWAY
SINGLE
CHILD'S TICKET

You may now pass the barrier below.

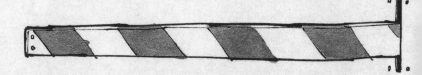

DESTINATIONS

ALL ABOARD!

PLATFORM ONE

· MORE PLEASE! ·

If you've been to Izzambard once, you'll want to go again. And again. And again. You'll be annoyed if you can't. That's why Ella and Leo were feeling a bit gloomy. They wanted more adventures. They wanted to go back and see their friends, Prince Bartholomew Buckle and Cogg the robot. They didn't want to just 'brush their teeth', 'tidy their bedrooms', and 'go to the park'.

'What's the matter with you two?' Mr

Leggit asked. He was carrying a hammer and some picture frames. 'You both look like a wet weekend.'

Leo groaned.

Ella groaned, too.

'We thought you liked our new house?' Mrs Leggit said.

'We do,' Leo replied.

'Yeah. We LOVE it,' Ella said.

'Then what's up?'

Ella sniffed. 'The Sleeping Key isn't working. So we can't get back into the Kingdom of Izzambard. And we promised that we would. And . . . oh, it's just awful.'

Mr and Mrs Leggit looked at Leo. Leo shrugged. He knew they didn't believe them. They'd laughed when he'd shown

them the Sleeping Key. It hadn't done anything. Not even yawned. It had just looked like an ordinary key. So he wasn't going to do that again. Mr and Mrs Leggit thought they'd made the whole thing up. To be honest, he was beginning to think so, too.

Mrs Leggit put her hands on her hips and sighed. 'Well, if you two can't find something to put a smile on your faces indoors, then you'd better go out. Go on. Off with you. Outside.' She shooed them out of the front door like they were a couple of pigeons.

'But what about my coat?' Ella asked.

'You don't need a coat,' Mrs Leggit said. 'It's nice out. In fact, you don't really need that big old red hat.'

Ella grabbed her hat with both hands and held it on tight. No one was going to

take her hat away. Ever.

'Come on, Ella.' Leo took her hand.
'Let's go back to the workshop and give
the door one more try.'

PLATFORM TWO

· HAMMERS AND DOORS ·

The inside of the workshop was dusty like a museum. It was full of exciting things, and I'd like to be able to tell you that Leo and Ella were excited. Tingling with anticipation. Full of happiness and 'Gosh!'

But they weren't.

That's because they'd tried to open the door to Izzambard lots of times and the magical Sleeping Key hadn't worked. In fact, they were beginning to think that

the Sleeping Key was no use at all. It
wouldn't so much as wriggle.

'This really is the last time,' Leo
warned, taking the Sleeping Key out of
his pocket. He stroked it. He patted it. He
even nibbled it. No. Nothing. It wouldn't
wake up!

Ella was getting desperate. 'Throw it.
Jump on it. Drop it on the floor.'

'I can't do that! I might kill it!'

'You've already nibbled it,' Ella said.
'And anyway, you can't kill keys.'

'Not normal ones,' Leo agreed. 'But
the Sleeping Key isn't normal. It yawns.
And it sniffs. And it wriggles and sighs. So
I don't want to kill it by accident.'

Ella nodded. Leo was right. Again. 'Try
the numbers in the lock.'

'We've tried that loads. 11.61 just
doesn't open the door like it did last time.

Not when the time on the clock doesn't match.' Leo shook the key. 'And this useless thing just won't move.'

'Leo. We've got to think of something. We need to get back to Izzambard. What if Griselda is destroying more Old Magic and hurting our friends?'

Leo felt panic in his tummy. Ella was right. The Clockmaker was wicked and out of control. They needed to get back. Fast. Leo stared at the clock hopefully. But it just said 4.35p.m. Normal time. Not a weird Izzambardian time like before.

'I'm good at finding things. Perhaps I'll find another magical object in here.' Ella started grabbing some of the things lying about the workshop and banging them on the floor. A bucket of coal. An iron spade. A golden birdcage.

CLANG. CLATTER. BASH.

'Careful!' Leo shouted. 'You'll break them!'

BANG. WALLOP. CRASH.

'Ella! Stop it!'

Ella stopped. Wait—she could hear a noise.

TAP. TAP. TAP.

TAPPETY TAP.

'What is that?' Leo asked.

'A tapping noise,' Ella answered.

'I know that. But where did it come from?'

Ella jumped up onto the boxes, trying to find it.

'Get down!' Leo said. 'You'll hurt yourself.'

'But I can hear it! It's so close!'

TAP. TAP. TAP. TAPPETY TAP.

'It's in there!' Ella pointed. It was coming from the trunk labelled '**LOST**'.

Leo took a deep breath. Anything could be inside. A spider. A rat. An enormous mechanical spider! An enormous mechanical spider sitting on top of a mechanical rat! Absolutely anything! But big brothers can't show fear. (It's one of the 'big brother' rules.) So Leo didn't. He knelt down and opened the lid.

Inside, was . . .

Just another box!

TAP. TAP. TAP.

Leo paused. He felt sick.

'Can I open it? Can I?' Ella asked.

Leo looked at Ella. Then, he remembered the second 'big brother' rule: 'Always let your little sister do the things you don't want to do.'

'Sure,' he said, getting up and standing aside.

TAP. TAP. TAP.

Ella pushed the brim of her hat out of
her eyes and opened the lid of the smaller
box. A flash of sunlight made her turn
away. Only, it wasn't a flash of sunlight—
it was the tappetty thing inside the box
inside the box.

'It's a tiny, shiny hammer!'

TAP TAP TAP BLINKETTY BLINK
TAP TAP TAP

It was a beautiful, glistening hammer.
Just like the one Mr Leggit was using back
at the house. Actually, what am I talking
about? It was NOTHING like the one Mr
Leggit was using back at the house. It was
much, much smaller. And prettier. And
full of light. And MOVING! Yes. How
could you not notice that it was moving?
Tapping against the side of the box
(inside the box), all on its own!

Ella picked it up—it was no bigger than
the palm of her hand. And remember,
Ella's hand was only eight years old, so
not really very big.

'DON'T TOUCH IT!' Leo shouted.

'Why not?'

'Because you don't know what it is!'

'It's a hammer,' Ella said. The hammer stopped moving. 'Aw. Look. I think it likes me.'

'Hammers don't "like" people, Ella.'

'They do if they're from Izzambard,' said Ella.

Leo remembered the Snarkifying Glass from their last adventure. He wasn't sure if the magical magnifying glass had liked him, but it had definitely 'hummed' more when it was cross or excited. Which was most of the time.

Ella had found a piece of old string. 'Look, if I wrap the top of the hammer with this string, I can wear it like a pretty necklace. It will go ever so nicely with my red hat.'

Ella hooked it around her neck.

13

'What if it's a dangerous object?' Leo asked.

Ella waved her hand in a 'don't be silly' way. 'Of course it isn't dangerous. It's a magical object, Leo. Prince Barty told us about them. It won't hurt us but we've got to return it to Izzambard.'

'Yes. You're probably right.' Leo still looked doubtful. 'But how can we when we can't open the door to

the railway platform?
The code and the
clock still don't
match.'

**TAP TAP TAP
BLINKETTY FLASH
TAP TAP TAP**

'Ouch! The hammer thing is moving!'
Suddenly, Ella had an idea. She pointed
the tip of the hammer directly at the
clock, and a huge beam of light burst out
of it.

'Look!' Leo pointed at the hands
whizzing round. Suddenly, they both
stopped.

11.61.

'Yes! The clock and the code match!' Leo said. 'It must work now!'

A little flash of light flickered out of the hammer as they ran towards the door. Leo twiddled with the combination lock and put in the numbers.

11:61

It worked! **PING!** The rusty lock sprang open. And so did the workshop's back door! The children tumbled onto the platform.

'Thank you, hammer,' Ella said, politely. The hammer flashed three times.

'Looks like we're right on time!' Leo said. For there it was, puffing through the steam: Prince Barty on his squirrel-powered, plum-coloured, Izzambardian train!

CHOOOOOOO CHOOOOOOOO!

PLATFORM THREE

· THE INCREDIBLE CRYSTALLATOR ·

'THE TRAIN NOW ARRIVING AT PLATFORM ONE IS THE 11.61 IZZAMBARD EXPRESS. STOPPING AT SNARKSVILLE, GOBLINORA BRIDGE, THE CRYSTAL CAVES...' The voice suddenly stopped. Prince Bartholomew, or Barty as he preferred to be called, had just spotted his Warm Heart friends on the platform! He leapt back into the main carriage and shouted out of the window: 'Leo! Ella! You're back! Quick. Hop on

board. And be careful of G . . . G . . .
Griselda's creeping vines in case they
trap you!'

CREEEEAAK

The glistening metal vines
that clung to the edges of the
platform had started to move. Leo
and Ella took one look at them, and
quickly jumped on board the train.

'Full Steam Ahead!' Barty shouted.
The train started to gain in speed and
Leo knew that the two noble waistcoated
squirrels, Lord and Lady Asquith, must
be working hard to stoke the engine. Leo
peered out of the window.

'We've beaten the vines. They've given
up.' Leo grinned as the metal creepers
collapsed back onto the platform.

'Well, I must say you haven't been gone
very long!' said Barty, wiping his forehead

19

with his hankie. 'We th . . . th . . . thought you'd be an age.'

'We were,' Ella replied.

'No you weren't!' Barty smiled. 'Cogg! Be so k . . . k . . . kind as to bring some whizzle-ade.' A strange-looking vacuum cleaner with wheels, cogs, and a sunroof wobbled into the carriage. (For those of you that don't already know, Cogg was Barty's loyal friend and the only talking vacuum cleaner in Izzambard.) His lights flashed and he spun around. Then he disappeared, and just as quickly, reappeared with two bottles of whizzle-ade with straws.

Leo had forgotten just how good it tasted.

Now, even though he was mostly clockwork and wasn't supposed to have Warm Heart feelings, Cogg had really missed the children and started to lightly vacuum Leo's cheek.

Leo knew Cogg meant well so tried his very best not to mind.

'But *slurp* we really *slurp* have been *slurp* ages,' Ella insisted.

'Weeks, in fact,' said Leo, pulling Cogg's nozzle off his face. 'We thought you'd be worried. In trouble, perhaps?'

'Trouble? We've b . . . b . . . barely had time to wash our socks!' Barty exclaimed.

'Socks?' Cogg was confused. 'I don't wear socks.'

'Nor do I,' said Barty, wriggling his toes. 'But I'm trying to speak Other World. Anyway, you've only b . . . b . . . been gone a day but I know what must have happened. Other World time stops when you come here. But our time stops or slows down when you go home. I think. Unless G . . . G . . . Griselda's been playing about with time in Izzambard again? Oh dear. Maybe that's it? One never really knows.'

'It doesn't matter,' Ella said. 'I don't understand time, anyway. Even when it does what it's supposed to do. But I do understand hammers. Look! It's full

of light.' She waved her little hammer
necklace at them all.

Barty gasped. 'Well, blow me down
and call me a will-o'-the-wisp! It's the
Incredible Crystallator! Wherever did you
find it?'

Leo blinked. 'The what?'

'Incredible Crystallator.' Ella beamed
at the hammer with pride. 'We found it in
our workshop at home. In a box inside
a box.'

'Look. Never mind about that,' Leo said. 'What I want to know is if the hammer is dangerous.'

'No. Well, n . . . n . . . not in the right hands.' Barty adjusted his train guard's cap and looked thoughtful.

'Are my hands the right hands?' Ella asked, looking at her fingers.

'Definitely.' Barty sighed. 'But the Incredible Crystallator would be dangerous in G . . . G . . . Griselda's hands. She would use its powers to destroy all the Old Magic in the Kingdom. That's all I meant. It should be in the hands of Gripendulum, the High Chief Hob Goblin of the Crystal Caves.'

'Gripendulum must be very small,' said Leo, looking at the tiny hammer.

'Of course he's not "very small". He's the High Chief of the Hob Goblins!'

'Well, his hammer is very small.' Leo looked at the shining object dangling around Ella's neck. A tiny blue clockwork butterfly fluttered past.

'Shhh! G . . . G . . . Griselda's spies!' Barty leant closer and whispered, 'Things aren't always what they seem, Leo. This is Izzambard, remember.' Barty's voice rose to a normal pitch. 'Cogg. Would you be so kind as to debutterfly the carriage?'

'Of course, Your Highness.' Cogg swivelled a nozzle and blew out a huge stream of blue air. The butterfly clattered to the floor. Then, it flew out of the window dizzily. 'Debutterflying complete,' said Cogg. But Barty had disappeared.

PLATFORM FOUR

·THE DARK STORM·

'DUE TO UNFORESEEN
CIRCUMSTANCES, THIS TRAIN WILL
BE GOING STRAIGHT THROUGH TO
THE CRYSTAL CAVES. APOLOGIES
FOR ANY INCONVENIENCE CAUSED.'

'Why does he do that?' Leo asked,
looking up at the tannoy. 'There's no one
else on the train.'

'I don't know.' Ella looked down the
carriage. 'Maybe he's talking to the
butterflies? Or Lord and Lady Asquith?

Or invisible things?'

'You're right!' Leo said. 'After all, this is Izzambard.'

Barty rushed back. 'The thing is,' he said, 'you'll need to return the Incredible Crystallator to Gripendulum, the High Chief of the Hob Goblins, so they can start mining again.' Barty shook his head sadly. 'Since the Fairy Dust mines closed down there's b . . . b . . . barely any magic left in this part of Izzambard now. It's a problem for the whole Kingdom.'

'Why?' asked Ella.

'Why?!' Barty exclaimed. 'Because that's how magic is fuelled. Fairy Dust. I thought every one knew that. Even Warm Hearts.'

Leo muttered something about Tinkerbell and said he knew about Fairy Dust already. But Ella wasn't really sure

he did. Not that it mattered. Not really.
Not when . . . there was an ENORMOUS
viaduct coming up straight ahead!

(For those of you who don't know
what a viaduct is, do let me explain.
It's a railway bridge with hundreds of
arches below—made entirely out of
shimmering crystal. Well, actually,
that's not quite true. In the

Other World, they're a bit different.
Fewer arches and made out of stone. But
Leo and Ella weren't in the Other World
now. And nor are you.)

'Wow! Look at that!' Ella blinked. 'I LOVE bridges! Especially ones that go over amazing valleys and in between massive mountains.'

The plum-coloured train was tiny compared to the towering crags and snow-topped peaks. Leo and Ella just couldn't stop staring out of the window.

Suddenly, the Incredible Crystallator started to shine.

'Take it off!' Leo said. 'It'll hurt your eyes.'

Ella yanked the shining beam of hammer from her neck and sat on it. (Not really the best idea. But Ella couldn't think what else to do.)

'Are we going over that bridge, Barty?' asked Leo. 'Is it strong enough? Won't it crack?'

'Crack!?' laughed Barty. 'Who ever heard of Goblinora Crystal cracking? It's the strongest material known to Izzambard. It's even stronger than a unicorn's horn.' Cogg's sunroof flipped up and down and Barty laughed again.

Leo didn't like being laughed at. It's not really fair when people laugh at you because you don't know something. Especially when you're trying your best to be a big brother. Leo folded his arms and huffed.

'Are you sure it's not going to crack?' Ella asked as Goblinora Bridge drew closer. 'It looks like it's made of ice.'

'Of course not!' said Barty. 'It was built in the time of Old Magic. When the Clockmakers, Royal Engineers, and Fairy Folk all worked side by side. As long as Goblinora Bridge is painted with a coat of Fairy Dust after each Dark Storm, it remains unbreakable.'

CHOOOOOOO CHOOOOOOOO!

Leo leant out of the window. He was sure he could see some cracks in the ice. Tiny spiderwebs of cracks, spreading across the arches ahead. An ice wind stung the tips of Leo's ears and he pulled his head back into the carriage. 'Barty, I thought that Fairy Dust was running out in this part of the Kingdom? That the mines had closed. And I'm sure I can see some cracks. When exactly was the last Dark Storm?'

Barty froze.

BLINKETTY BLINK. FLASH. BLINKETTY BLINK.

'Your bottom is flashing, Ella,' Cogg said.

'And it feels a bit warm!' Ella shuffled

off the Incredible Crystallator.

Leo tried again: 'When was the last Dark Storm?'

Barty dabbed his forehead with his hanky and looked like he was going to be sick. 'The last Dark Storm was last night.' Then he screamed: 'STOP THE TRAIN!'

But it was too late.

CRAAAAAAAAAACCCK!

PLATFORM FIVE

· THE ANGERWICK ·

Leo exploded like a firework in the sky. 'WHAT? YOU MEAN THIS BRIDGE MIGHT COLLAPSE? WE MIGHT ALL DIE?'

'I'm af . . . af . . . afraid so,' Barty stammered.

KERPLUNK. One of Cogg's nozzles fell on the floor. (He always fell apart when he panicked.)

Ella clutched the Incredible Crystallator to her chest.

'REVERSE THE TRAIN,' Leo said.

'We can't,' Cogg replied.

'Why?'

'Squirrel-powered engines never go backwards. Their tails always get in the way.'

Leo didn't understand, but there was no time to argue.

'I want to go home!' Ella screamed.

Leo peered out of the window, the icy wind racing through his hair. He looked down. The drop into the valley made his stomach lurch.

If the bridge broke, they would all
definitely plunge to their deaths.

CRAAAAAAAAAACCCK

The bridge was straining under the
weight of the train.

CHOOOOOOO CHOOOOOOOO!

Leo pulled his head back into the
carriage again. 'If anything happens to
my sister, I'll—'

He didn't need to finish. Barty knew
exactly what Leo meant.

'Oh. It's all m . . . m . . . my fault. But
please don't panic. We might still make
it.'

'Might?!' cried Ella, pulling her hat
over her eyes. (Ella was normally very
brave. But plunging to your death
because of a shortage of Fairy Dust,
while returning an Incredible Crystallator
to a Hob Goblin, would scare even the

bravest of Warm Hearts. Even I would have been a little afraid.)

CREEEEEEAAAAEAAAAAK

'Well we're n . . . n . . . nearly across the bridge. It's only another seventeen trundlegrinds long,' Barty said.

'What's a trundlegrind?' Leo asked.

'About thirty whippits.'

Leo sighed. However long it was, the end of Goblinora Bridge was nowhere in sight.

Then the train began to slow down.

'What's happening?' asked Leo. 'Why are we losing speed?'

'It's the Asquiths,' Barty said. 'They must be getting tired, but the shovels only work properly for the squirrels so there's nothing we can do to help.'

Leo frowned. 'We need a plan.' Now, Leo didn't know he was good at 'plans'.

37

And definitely not 'fast' ones. (Lots of us are like that. We don't know we're good at things until we're in a tight spot.) But Leo's 'planning' bits were tingling into action. He felt full of electricity. 'Is there any Fairy Dust on the train?' Leo asked. 'Any at all?'

'Yes. Yes there is!' said Barty. 'I have a tiny private supply in my luggage rack.'

'Right. Then get it. Quick. We can mix it with some whizzle-ade to make it spread further, and Cogg can use one of his nozzles to paint it on the bridge. We'll need to do it from the front of the train, so we can paint the coat of Fairy Dust before the weight of the heavy carriages makes Goblinora Bridge crumble. Hurry. There's no time to lose.'

'WHEEEEEEEEBBBBIBBBBLELOP,' Cogg said in agreement.

Within what seemed like seconds, Barty had disappeared and returned with three bottles of whizzle-ade and two tiny pots of Fairy Dust.

'Right.' Leo took a deep breath. 'Let's dangle Cogg out of the window.'

'What?' blurted out Cogg. 'Dangle me out of where?'

Barty stroked Cogg's sunroof and whispered, 'You can do it, Cogg. For Izzambard. For us. For *me*.'

Cogg's middle section swivelled. 'All right, Your Highness. I'll do it for you.'

Barty smiled as he mixed the pots of Fairy Dust into the whizzle-ade. It shone like sunlight trapped in sea. Then, very carefully, Ella helped Cogg dip his nozzle into one of the bottles.

TAP TAP TAP

Ella had almost forgotten about the
Incredible Crystallator. She had looped it
around her neck again. It seemed excited.
Perhaps it was the Fairy Dust? Perhaps
it was the crystal bridge. There were too
many 'perhapses' but no time to think.

CRAAAAAAAAAACCCK

Leo and Barty ran to the engine room
past brave Lord and Lady Asquith who
were still shovelling, and hoisted Cogg out
of the window.

'Are you sure Cogg w . . . w . . . will be s . . . s . . . safe?' Barty asked, clutching one of Cogg's bottom wheels.

Leo didn't answer as Cogg's remaining nozzles swung out of the train. He didn't know. He'd never done anything like this before.

CHOOOOOOO CHOOOOOOOO!

Cogg swung upside down from the window, painting the bridge as fast as he could. Ella dangled a bottle out of the window too, so he could dip his nozzle into it when he needed more.

Slowly, the glistening white crystal bridge stopped **CREAKING**. With every brush of paint, it seemed to **FIZZLE** back into strength.

CHOOOOOOO CHOOOOOOOO!

They were nearly at the other side! 'You've done it, Cogg! You've done it!' They pulled him back in as the plum-coloured train edged towards the mountain.

'Wait!' Cogg cried. But it was too late. One of his nozzles had got caught on the window's edge and tumbled down into the abyss. They watched as it clattered against the sides of the rocks. Further and further it fell.

'STOP THE TRAIN!' shouted Barty. 'We need to get Cogg's nozzle back.'

SCREEEEEEEEECCCHHHHHHHHH

The train came to a stop.

CLANG. CLATTER. CRASH.

There was a moment of silence.

CLINK.

The nozzle had just reached the bottom of the valley.

But then, there was a most unexpected...

Roaaaarrrrr!

The train shook. Barty, Leo, and Ella
couldn't help it—they all SCREAMED.
The side of the valley was moving! Part
of the rock face was peeling away! Only
it wasn't a rock face. It was a GIANT,
his beard made out of tree roots,
his face a lump of
carved grey
rock.

'HIDE!' shouted Leo, grabbing Ella and diving under the walnut table.

'It's j . . . j . . . just an Angerwick,' Barty said, almost calmly. 'We're s . . . safe. As long as we don't light his fuse.'

'Light his fuse?' Ella asked.

'Yes. Angerwicks are loyal to my family—the Buckle Crown. Have been for centuries. As long as you don't light their fuse.'

'But does the Angerwick know you're Prince Bartholomew Buckle?' Ella asked.

'Of course. The whole of Izzambard knows how I am cursed to drive this train. How the evil G . . . G . . . Griselda will imprison me on it for ever if it's even one minute late.'

'Good,' Leo said. 'I mean, not good. But good.'

Barty smiled sadly.

45

'And how do you light an Angerwick's fuse?' Ella asked.

'By making him cross,' said Barty.

Leo looked up. 'Cross? How? By dropping something on him? Like a nozzle?'

'Y . . . y . . . yes,' Barty replied.

Cogg blushed.

'YES!' Barty screamed.

Roaaaarrrrrr!

PLATFORM SIX

· THE GIANT'S PAIN ·

Barty leant out of the stationary train and shouted as loud as he could:

'Greetings, M . . . M . . . Most Honourable Angerwick. I am Prince Bartholomew Buckle, heir to the G . . . G . . . Great Throne of Izzambard, Defender of the Old Magic and Ally of the Angerwicks since time began.' Barty stopped and dabbed his face with his hankie. Ella looked at his hands. He was shaking like a leaf.

47

'And I am an Angerwick,' boomed the giant. 'Keeper of the Gates and Defender of the Bridge since Old Time began. Greetings, Royal Blood of Buckle. But which of your passengers woke me from my sleep of a hundred years? Which one dared to light my fuse? Roaaaarrrrr!'

'Oh no! It really is my fault!' Cogg swivelled his mid-section and conked out.

'Poor Cogg,' Ella said, stroking his sunroof. 'You're not to blame. You were being dangled upside down. And you were painting a bridge. And being a hero!'

Immediately, Cogg switched back on. But he didn't have time to feel heroic for long because the Angerwick had lifted an enormous boulder and was raising it over his head, ready to throw it at the train.

'Barty! How can we stop the Angerwick?' Leo screamed. 'What's his weakness?'

Barty's eyes flashed. 'There's only one weakness I can think of: Angerwicks get really creaky knees.'

'What?' It wasn't the answer Leo had been expecting.

Barty dabbed his forehead with his hankie. 'They say they're even more painful than Stippleroach bites. The only known cure is Fairy Dust, but I'm afraid we've used all ours to fix the bridge.'

Leo wasn't really sure why, but suddenly he felt that electricity again. It kept on happening whenever they were in trouble.

'ANGERWICK,' Leo shouted, leaning out of the carriage.

'What are you doing?!' Ella cried. But Leo took no notice.

'ANGERWICK. I am a Warm Heart. I understand your pain.'

'Understand my pain?' boomed the Angerwick.

'Yes. The pain of the Creaky Knee.'

The Angerwick groaned and began to weep. Tears like rivers poured from his eyes. Slowly, he lowered the boulder.

'You have seen well, Warm

50

Heart. But what can you do for the creaky knees of an Angerwick like me?'

'I can bring you Fairy Dust,' Leo shouted. 'To soothe your pain.'

The Angerwick laughed and the mountains shook. 'But there is no Fairy Dust being made in the Crystal Caves. My supplies have all run out. The Incredible Crystallator was stolen. The Hob Goblin mines are closed. We Angerwicks are left to suffer through Biting Winds and Dark Storms alone.'

'But I have the Incredible Crystallator,' Ella shouted, waving the hammer in the air. The Angerwick leant forwards, making the train shiver on the track.

'And we will return it to the High Chief Hob Goblin,' Barty promised, 'and he will reopen the mines. There will be enough Fairy Dust for every Angerwick in the land.'

Aaaaaahuuump

'Is he angry?' Ella asked. 'Have we lit his fuse again?'

'No,' Barty smiled. 'That is one of the most beautiful sounds in the Kingdom of Izzambard. It is the sound of an Angerwick calming down!'

'To go to sleep with no pain: this is all that an Angerwick dreams of.' The Angerwick put the boulder down. As he did so, the valley echoed with the sound of his knees and back going CRACK and CLICK.

'We will return.' Barty waved a royal

wave. 'We promise, by all that
is Buckle and Warm Heart.
And if you can please be
so kind as to give us the
metal fragment that fell
from the train and lit your
fuse, then we will deliver
a crate of Fairy Dust to your
mountainside.'

'A whole crate
of fairy dust?'
bellowed the Angerwick.
He laughed with delight
and a hot breeze of Angerwick breath
blew into the train. 'If you deliver
this I will not harm you. For I
will sleep like an Angerwick babe
for a thousand years.'

The valley roared with a crack of
thunder. Only it wasn't a crack of thunder.

It was the Angerwick's knees creaking as he bent down and picked up Cogg's tiny nozzle between forefinger and thumb. 'Here. Take this,' he said, passing it like a pinhead through the window of the train. The nozzle was all crushed and crumbled. 'As you have promised to stop an Angerwick's pain, I promise that I will give you safe passage and await your return. But if you break your promise . . .' The Angerwick paused. 'If you break your promise,' he repeated, more quietly, 'even I fear what I am capable of doing. For Angerwicks should never be wronged.'

Ella and Leo shivered as they watched the huge bulk of the Angerwick sink back into the mountainside.

'I can't even see him anymore!' Ella

said. 'Where is he?'

'There. Look. His beard is the grey
birch forest.'

'Wow!' Ella sighed.

The Asquiths had started to shovel
again, for the steam started hissing and the
train's whistle blew:

CHOOOOOOO CHOOOOOOOO!

The carriage was still warm with
Angerwick breath, so the smell of freshly
dug peat and rich mountain streams still
lingered in the air, but within what
seemed like seconds, Goblinora
Bridge and the giant were left
far behind.

PLATFORM SEVEN

· THE ANGERWICK'S BREATH ·

Ella yawned. 'Do we have to take the
Incredible Crystallator back now, Leo?'
she said. 'I really want to go to sleep.'

'Me too.' Leo stretched and lay
down across the seat. 'Let's take it back

tomorrow. Or maybe the next day. Or maybe the . . .'

Cogg tried to vacuum them both awake.

'WAKE UP!' Barty shook them both by the shoulders. 'Whatever you do, don't sleep!'

'We're tired,' Leo said, pushing Cogg's nozzle away. Barty pressed a bottle of whizzle-ade against Leo's dry mouth.

'Drink this! Quick! DO NOT SLEEP.'

Leo took a gulp. The bubbles went up his nose. It made him blink. Barty pressed the bottle against Ella's lips, too. She spluttered a bit and sat up.

Leo rubbed his eyes. 'What's happening to us?' he asked.

'It's the Angerwick,' Barty explained. 'Too much Angerwick breath makes young Warm Hearts sleep. But you

mustn't! Angerwick sleep can last for a
thousand years.'

'Whazzat?' Leo asked, drowsily.

'Z^z$_z^{z}_z$. . .' Ella was starting to nod off.
Leo's eyes began to close.

'Oh heavens!' exclaimed Barty. 'Quick.
They're f . . . f . . . falling asleep!' Barty
ran up and down the carriage, opening
all the windows to let in some fresh air as
well.

But still they yawned.

Barty looked at Cogg. 'Debutterfly
them.'

'But there aren't any butterflies,' Cogg
said.

'Just do it!'

Cogg did as he was told. He swivelled
his middle section around and covered
them with a burst of deep blue steam.

Ella and Leo coughed. At first, it made

them dizzy. But it seemed to do the trick. Slowly, they began to wake up. But they still looked like they'd been dragged out of bed.

'Oh d . . . d . . . dear!' said Barty. 'You both look d . . . d . . . dreadful. You'll never convince Gripendulum to reopen the mines looking like that!'

'Shall we go home then and come back another day?' Ella yawned.

'No,' Leo said. He'd read enough books and seen enough films to know that adventures don't work like that. 'We can't just stop and have a picnic! This is an adventure. We have to carry on and finish the job. Especially as we're on a squirrel-powered train and trying to return one of the magical objects of Izzambard to its rightful owner.'

Barty patted Leo on the back. 'My f . . . f . . . father would be proud of you,' he said. Leo smiled. He'd never met King Buckle. But he liked the idea of a king being proud of him.

Barty straightened his cap and looked out of the window. Ella leant on his shoulder and looked out, too. Everything was white. Not snow white, but crystal white. The towering grey Angerwick mountains had disappeared and been replaced with glimmering crystal surfaces that looked like jagged ice-cubes.

'It's a bit like the North Pole,' Ella said. 'But not cold.'

'That's because it's crystal, not ice.' Barty smiled.

'Where's the Fairy Dust?' Ella asked.

'Deep inside the white mountains.' Cogg wobbled over and vacuumed her back.

TAP TAP BLINKETTY FLASH TAP

'Oh!' Ella clutched the Incredible Crystallator. 'I think it wants to go home.' She stroked it and said, 'There, there.'

'Oh my g . . . goodness!' Barty exclaimed, dabbing his forehead with his hankie. 'I nearly forgot!' He jumped up and ran down the corridor.

'THIS TRAIN WILL SHORTLY
BE ARRIVING AT THE CRYSTAL
CAVES. PLEASE CHANGE HERE
FOR CONNECTIONS TO GRIFFIN
ISLAND.'

The engines began to hiss as the train
slowly came to a halt.

'Come on, everyone. Hurry. Let's
breathe some Angerwick-free air. We
need to get off.'

'We?' Ella asked. 'But you can't get off
the train, Barty. Not for long, anyway.
If the train runs late then Griselda will
know, and she'll make you stay on it for
ever.'

'That's right,' Leo agreed. 'Griselda
will unleash her terrible curse on you and
you'll never be king. You'll always be a
prisoner on a squirrel-powered train.'

'I know. B . . . b . . . but I'm fed up

of doing what G . . . G . . . Griselda
wants. And I'm getting off. Cogg is my
best friend and I need to get his nozzle
replaced.' He held up the crumpled
piece of metal. 'Look, it got completely
destroyed when it fell on the Angerwick's
toe.'

Cogg sniffled. 'But, Prince Barty,
you should stay on the train. It's too
dangerous.'

'I have m . . . m . . . made up my mind,'
said Barty. 'I may not be the b . . . b . . .
bravest prince, but I am a good friend.
So I will take Cogg to the Undergoblin's
Furnace while you find the High Chief
of the Hob Goblins. Just return the
Incredible Crystallator and he'll open the
mines again. And don't forget to bring a
crate of Fairy Dust back to the train so
that the Angerwick won't explode.'

63

Leo and Ella nodded.

'H . . . h . . . hurry then,' said Barty. 'The Asquiths will stay on board and make sure the train waits for all of us. And as soon as Cogg's nozzle is fixed and he's all put back together we will meet you back at the train.'

PLATFORM EIGHT

· THE FAIRY FEUDS ·

Prince Barty could barely remember the last time he'd stepped off the train. If you didn't know that it had been a very long time since he had last stood on a platform, you might have just thought he was doing an impression of a Warm Heart walking on the moon.

'Leo, look at the floor,' Ella said. 'It's sparkling like glitter.'

'It's made out of star grains.' Barty was smiling as he caught up with them. 'Some say the crystals came from Izzambardian stars. It's so good to be on solid ground again.'

'Star grains!' Ella sighed. It was the most beautiful thought. Crystals falling from the stars.

'Come on,' Leo said. 'We've got a lot to do!'

'Y . . . y . . . yes. Of course. You're right,' Barty said, heading north. 'Just keep south along the crystal path. It will lead you straight to the caves.'

'**WIBBLLLLEEEEEEE**' Cogg shouted. Leo and Ella waved, then ran until they left the train and the Asquiths far behind. Ella was glad she had the Incredible Crystallator and her hat with her. Somehow, they made her feel safe.

'Your hat looks very red,' Leo said, waiting for Ella to catch up.

'That's just because everything is white,' Ella replied. 'Haven't you noticed? Everything's been white for ages. All crystal and star-grain and sparkle.'

Leo was just about to say something very interesting about purples and blues and crystals in the Other World, when something made them both jump. Well, it wasn't really something, it was someone. Someone with lots of black feathers. But it wasn't a bird. (Well, definitely not a mechanical one.)

Leo pulled Ella behind a white rock.

'What is it?' she asked. They both stared. The black feathery winged thing was busy muttering to itself.

'If that stupid, stupid, silly Nut Snap doesn't do what I want him to do, then I'm just going to—'

The thing stopped. It had seen the tip

of a red feather sticking out from behind the rock. Ella's feather. The one on her hat.

'Oooo,' said the black feathery winged thing. 'I like red feathers. Red feathers are one of my favourite things.'

Ella held onto her hat. 'Why does everyone in Izzambard always want my hat? Someone is always trying to steal it.'

'Shhhhh!' Leo hissed.

Suddenly, the thing was peering down upon them. It must have flown up on to the rock.

'Hello,' it said. 'You are funny fairies. You have lost all your wings.'

'We're not fairies,' Leo answered. 'Are you?'

The black feathery winged thing didn't look like a fairy. At least, not like the ones in books. It had a big scar on the side of its face and hairs coming out of its chin.

'Of course I'm a fairy!' said the fairy, rearranging her black feathery crown. 'I'm Ice Splatter and I—'

'THERE YOU ARE! YOU STINKY BEAST!' Another fairy flipped through the sky and bopped Ice Splatter on the head with a silver birch branch, just missing Ella's face. This fairy was the colour of autumn leaves—a glow of oranges and browns. 'Sorry about that.' It paused and tilted its head. 'Oh. I like your red feathers,' it cooed.

Ella stepped backwards. This was not the sort of behaviour she expected from fairies. And she wished they'd stop looking at her hat. But she needn't have worried too much. Suddenly, the fairies were on top of each other, tumbling along the crystal-flecked floor in a ball.

'TAKE THAT, THUNDER PANTS,' yelled Nut Snap, yanking the hairs on Ice Splatter's chin.

70

'TAKE THAT FIRST, CLOT HEAD!'
shouted Ice Splatter, pulling out some of
Nut Snap's feathers.

'ENOUGH! Break it up!' Leo bellowed.
(For that's what the teachers did at
school.) Then he waded in and tried to
separate the fairies, who were now biting
the tips of each other's wings.

'You are not nice fairies,' shouted Ella.
Ice Splatter and Nut Snap stopped.

'Not nice fairies!' Ice Splatter shrieked.

'Not nice fairies?' Nut Snap cried.

'Of course we're nice fairies.' Ice Splatter stomped her feet.

'Yes. Of course we are,' Nut Snap said.

'No you're not,' said Ella. 'You fight and you bite and are mean.' The fairies looked at Leo. Leo nodded. The fairies looked at each other. Then, their bottom lips started to wobble and they both started to cry.

'The thing-with-no-wings called us "mean",' Ice Splatter stammered. 'We are not mean, are we, Nut Snap?'

'No. We are not mean,' Nut Snap replied, holding Ice Splatter's hand very tight. 'We are fairies. And we are the very best of friends.'

'Best friends?' Leo laughed. 'What? But you're biting each other!'

Nut Snap bawled: 'It's all the High Chief of the Hob Goblins' fault.'

'Yes,' Ice Splatter wailed. 'If he hadn't closed down the mine, and we hadn't run out of Fairy Dust, then my chin wouldn't be so hairy.'

'And my wings wouldn't be so heavy,' said Nut Snap. 'I am supposed to be as light as a winkleflit. But I'm as heavy as a thumplethwaite.'

'And without Fairy Dust, we forget our fairy manners. And we no longer feel ourselves. It's not just me and Nut Snap! Since the mines closed, all our fairy tribes are feuding. There's even been talk of Fairy War!' Both fairies hugged each other, fell on the floor, and wept.

'Now, now,' Ella said. 'There's no need

to cry. I'm sure we'll work something out.'

BOOOO HOOOOOOOOOOOO

Their cries got louder and louder.

'What do we do, Leo?'

'I'm thinking,' he said.

TAP TAP BLINKETTY FLASH

Suddenly, the fairies stopped crying.
They picked themselves up and flew over
to Ella's side at the speed of light.

'It's the Incredible Crystallator! You
have the Incredible Crystallator!'

'I know,' Ella said, holding on to her necklace tight.

Ice Splatter beamed.

BLINK BLINKETTY FLASH BLINK

Nut Snap's fingers reached for the hammer around Ella's neck but Leo flicked him away. 'We need to take it to the High Chief of the Hob Goblins,' Leo said. 'Then he'll reopen the mines.'

Nut Snap threw himself on the floor. 'No he won't! He'll never reopen anything.'

'He is even more horrible than that!' said Ice Splatter. 'I wish Gripendulum had never been made the High Chief.'

Nut Snap and Ice Splatter both started bawling again. 'Oh, Ice Splatter,' Nut Snap cried. 'More hairs growing on your chin! And my wings! They feel even heavier!'

75

'More hairs? Heavier? Nothing will ever be all right again!'

'Let me pull them out for you.' Nut Snap yanked Ice Splatter's latest whiskers.

'Ouch!' Ice Splatter screamed with pain. 'And I'll make you lighter, you great big clumsy nitwit!' She hurled herself on top of Nut Snap and tried to tug out his wing feathers.

'Stop it!' Nut Snap yelled. They started to roll around the floor again, screaming and spitting feathers across the path.

'Come on, Ella,' said Leo. 'We're wasting time. If we don't return the Incredible Crystallator, there'll be a Fairy War. We need to get the goblin mines open. This land needs Fairy Dust. Now!'

PLATFORM NINE

· MINERS OF THE MONARCHY ·

You may have wondered why Griselda, the evil Clockmaker, had not appeared in Leo and Ella's journey to the Crystal Caves. But the thing is, she already had! Like all wicked rulers, she was everywhere. She was behind the Dark Storm. She made Goblinora Bridge crack. She knew all about the brewing Fairy War. And she knew about the children and their plans. She needed to stop them getting into the mine, or else

she would begin to lose her power over
the Kingdom.

In most parts of
Izzambard, Griselda's
mechanical birds (the
heronites) roamed
the skies—dropping
their oil on Fairy Dust Markets
and destroying Old Magic wherever they
could. But the birds were no good in the
hidden and twisting depths

of the Crystal Caves. Her
flying spies could be seen
against the blanket-white
sky and couldn't enter
the twisting tunnels of the
earth. That's why she'd been so busy
creating new things. New things that
she'd just given to some creatures from
Old Times. And one of those creatures,

wearing their 'new thing' was just about to appear—right before Ella and Leo's eyes.

'What's that?' asked Ella. Right in front of them was a patch of shifting shadow. Moving. Like a ripple of wave in snow.

'I don't know.' Leo stopped. 'Don't touch it.'

'It doesn't look sharp,' Ella replied.

'Still don't touch it.'

Ella didn't. They watched as the strange lump moved around the ground. Suddenly, other lumps in the twinkling, star-grained earth started to move, too. Leo didn't feel safe. 'Quick! Let's hide behind this tree.'

They crouched down under some silver branches and watched. Strange glistening heads started to appear in the floor! Like . . . wait . . . Like moles—wearing strange mechanical monocles!

'WOW! I LOVE m—' But Leo had put

his hand over Ella's mouth just in time. A mole's head surfaced and looked around.

'All clear, chaps,' it said. About eighteen other faces popped up out of the ground. 'Right ho, Sergeant. Time to touch base with the Leader—monocles on.' All the moles fiddled with a switch on the side of their monocles with their tiny paws. Leo and Ella gasped as a hologram of Griselda appeared on a face of white rock.

'MINERS OF THE MONARCHY,'
Griselda's voice boomed. Ella trembled.
The hologram seemed to be looking
straight at her.

'Don't worry. It's just a hologram. She
can't see you,' said Leo.

But Ella wasn't so sure. Griselda's gaze
seemed to pierce right through her. She
pulled the brim of her hat over her eyes.

'PREPARE FOR ACTION. Now that
you have tried and tested your monocles,
you are ready to do my glorious work.
You are no longer blind and helpless
in the earth. You are MECHANICAL
MOLES—with eyes as sharp as griffins'.'

The mechanical moles all cheered.

Griselda looked so beautiful, Leo nearly
cheered too!

'Enough! Quiet!' The moles stopped.

'The Butterflies have reported that the

83

Wicked Warm Hearts DELIBERATELY
LIT THE FUSE OF THE ANGERWICK!'

The mechanical moles gasped.

'Not only that, they have already
caused a fairy feud! It may well lead to
FAIRY WAR and it will be all the Warm
Hearts' fault!'

The moles gasped again.

'And if you don't block the entrances
to THE CRYSTAL CAVES, they will try
to destroy the Kingdom's final stores of
Fairy Dust. THOSE CHILDREN MUST
BE STOPPED!'

'Hear, hear!' cheered the moles.

'Then what are you waiting for?'
yelled Griselda. 'MINERS OF THE
MONARCHY. DISPERSE AND BLOCK
THE ENTRANCES. NOW!'

The moles all disappeared like
bubbles into sand. Griselda's hologram

disappeared, too.

'Did you hear that?' Ella asked. 'She called us "Wicked Warm Hearts".'

'I know.' Leo nodded.

'She said we'd lit the Angerwick's fuse on purpose and started the fairy feud.'

'I know.'

'And she said we're going to destroy the Kingdom's Fairy Dust.'

'I know,' Leo said. Ella stroked the Incredible Crystallator. It made her feel better, somehow.

'But why did Griselda say that? It's not even the truth.'

'Because she needs the moles to believe in her,' Leo explained. They're not made completely out of clockwork, like the heronites. It's just their monocles that she created: they are loyal to her because she has helped them to see. And she is

85

beautiful. But if they find out that she's not beautiful on the inside, then they'll be hard to control. So she must make them believe that she is good, and make them believe we're bad. Even if it means telling lies. It's what evil clever leaders do best.'

'But do lies actually work?'

'No. Not normally. People usually see through them.'

'But the moles can only see through Griselda's mechanical monocles! So they'll believe everything she says.'

Leo looked thoughtful. 'Not if they switch them off,' he said.

PLATFORM TEN

·THE ICY WILDS·

Meanwhile, back at the Undergoblin's Furnace, Cogg was feeling much more himself. His crumpled nozzle had been fixed and all his loose bits had been firmly screwed back on.

'I can't thank you enough, goblins,' said Barty. The goblins all bowed low. Since the High Chief of the Hob Goblins had locked himself in his cave, they'd missed bowing to someone important.

'Is there anything else we can do for you, my princeliness?' They all bowed again.

'Well, actually, there is,' Barty replied.

'What is it, my regal lord? How may we help?'

'Cogg and I need to rush back to the train, but could you go and help the High Chief? He'll be needing workers.'

'Our High Chief?' asked a goblin, spanner still in hand. 'But he has disowned us. He has closed our mines. He has forbidden us from digging any Fairy Dust. He won't even let us bow to him!'

'I know it's been hard,' Barty replied. 'But things are changing. There are brave Warm Hearts heading to the Crystal Caves—determined to return the Incredible Crystallator. They need your help. If they are successful in their quest, goblin miners will be needed so that Gripendulum can return you all to Hob Goblin glory times. Your courage will be spoken of throughout the land.'

The goblins all bowed so low that their faces touched the floor.

'Former glory times?!' they whispered. 'The Incredible Crystallator! Back at the Crystal Caves? Can such a thing be true?'

'Yes, yes, yes!' said Cogg, eagerly. (He was feeling so much better!)

Suddenly, there was a strange clinking in the air. A swarm of blue butterflies had flown into the entrance of the Undergoblin's Furnace.

'Ouch! Ouch! Ouch!' Barty yelled, as they crashed into his face, stinging his cheeks and eyes. 'Debutterfly them, Cogg!' he shouted.

Cogg blasted some blue steam at Barty's head. The butterflies fell to the floor, and then flew away dizzily.

'G . . . G . . . Griselda knows where I am!' Barty said. 'She's angry. She only sends sw . . . sw . . . swarms when she's angry. It's a w . . . w . . . warning. What will she do to me?!'

Cogg tried to be as brave as a talking vacuum can be. 'Prince. She will not hurt you. Not while I'm here with all my nozzles intact.'

Barty dabbed his forehead with his hankie and smiled. 'I am a very lucky prince. Now, p . . . p . . . please goblins, go with all speed to help the Warm Hearts. Cogg and I m . . . must return to the train.'

* * *

Ella and Leo were following the crystal path, hoping that the Gripendulum's cave wasn't far away, when Ella's biggest fear actually happened. Yes. That's right!

Someone stole her hat!

'Leo!' she squealed. 'It's gone!'

'What's gone?'

'My hat!' She grabbed at the place
it had once been. They both watched,
helpless, as it bobbed into the distance:
a deep red blob floating against the
glistening, star-grain-flecked, white
rock.

'What took it?' Leo asked. 'Was
it the wind?'

'No. There is no wind.'

They both saw a
little flash of light—no,
little drops of light
that fizzed, then
disappeared.

Ella had seen them before: in a fairy tale about a princess and a wood. 'It's a will-o'-the-wisp. You have to follow them. Or maybe you're not meant to follow them? I can't remember. But look. It's sooo pretty.'

Before Leo could stop her, Ella had run off the crystal path, and was following the flickering light through the white birch woods.

'Don't leave the path!' shouted Leo. But it was too late. So Leo did what big brothers always have to do: he ran after her.

When he caught up, Ella was standing underneath an enormous silver tree, shouting at her hat in the air. 'You are a very, very, very naughty will-o'-the-wisp. Give me my hat back!'

'How do you know it's a will-o'-the-wisp?' Leo asked.

'Because of the fizzing lights.'

'I see.' Leo nodded. 'Give my sister her hat back.' He tried to jump up and grab it in the air. But the hat floated away. They both chased it.

It floated through woods and past streams until it took them down a steep path towards a big rushing river.

'I don't like this,' Leo said.

Ella saw a flicker of red: her hat was hovering by the entrance of a cave. Then, like a disappearing fish, it darted inside.

'Hang on.' Leo looked around. 'I

think the will-o'-the-wisp might have led us here on purpose. The crystal path probably led to the entrances that the moles had closed. But this cave looks open. Perhaps it's the only way into the mines?'

TAP TAP TAP TAPPETY TAP

The Incredible Crystallator was getting excited.

'Perhaps the High Chief of the Hob Goblins is close?'

'Maybe,' Ella replied. The cave was dripping with water. It was also full of darkness, but with the fizzing pulse of light and the red hat bobbing in the air before them, they clutched each other's hands and followed it inside.

PLATFORM ELEVEN

· CUTHBERT THE CAVE WORM ·

When you follow a will-o'-the-wisp into
a cave, you know something weird is
going to happen. Especially when you've
already met a fairy with a hairy chin and
are looking for the High Chief of the
Hob Goblins. That's why Leo wasn't that
surprised by what he saw. Bear with me.
It's not easy to explain.

The pulse of the will-o'-the-wisp
disappeared, but just around the second
twist in the cave's entrance, there was a

cavern full of deep pink light.

'Wow!' said Ella. 'It's like a dream.'

Leo nodded and sighed. (His dreams were mostly about electricity. And in his dreams, electricity was green and blue. But actually, at that moment, he realized that deep pink was the most electric colour he'd ever seen.)

'GO BACK,' said a strange gravelly voice. It echoed off the walls of the cave.

'Who's that?' Leo asked, peering into the pink.

'I AM CUTHBERT THE CAVE WORM, GUARDIAN OF THE CRYSTAL CAVES. GRIPENDULUM DOES NOT WISH TO SEE YOU. HE DOES NOT WISH TO SEE ANYONE. THE WILL-O'-THE-WISP SHOULD NEVER HAVE LED YOU HERE.'

Ella couldn't see him, but she didn't like

the sound of a 'cave worm'. Cuthbert's voice was much louder than any worm's should be.

'But we need to save the Kingdom of Izzambard.' Leo was trying hard to be brave. 'We need to return the Incredible Crystallator to Gripendulum. We need him to reopen the mines.'

Cuthbert slunk into the light and bumped into the wall. He wasn't as big as Leo and Ella were expecting, but he was

just big enough to wear Ella's red hat—
even though it kept slipping over his eyes.

'Give me my hat back!' Ella stomped
her foot.

'ONLY IF YOU GO BACK,' shouted
Cuthbert, wriggling over to the other side
of the cave.

'We can't,' Leo said. 'The Angerwick
will explode, Fairy War will begin, the evil
Clockmaker will rule Izzambard for ever,
the Old Magic will be destroyed, and

Prince Buckle will never get to go home!'

'OH. WELL, IN THAT CASE . . .'
Cuthbert shivered and lowered his head.
Ella grabbed her hat while she had the
chance. It felt a bit sticky, but she put it on
anyway.

'YOU MUST GO THIS WAY.' He
wiggled his tail in the direction of an even
deeper pink cave.

'Why are you shouting?' Ella asked.

'I AM NOT SHOUTING,' shouted
Cuthbert.

Ella giggled.

'Well, thank you for showing us where
to go,' Leo said, glad to get away. 'And
goodbye.'

Cuthbert slunk into the darkness.

'Cave worms are funny,' Ella said.

'They're definitely very shouty,' Leo
replied. He smiled and grabbed Ella's

hand as they walked into the second cavern. The will-o'-the-wisp had gone and the pink sea of light seemed to flicker on and off. They walked and walked and walked. But nothing seemed to change. They didn't seem to be getting anywhere. In fact, Leo was sure he'd seen the same dark pink rock a hundred times.

'Ella, put your hat on that rock.'

'No!' Ella said, clutching it tight.

'Just for a minute. I want to do an experiment. Put it on that rock, and I promise we'll come back for it.'

Ella screwed up her face, but did as she was told.

'Now,' Leo said, 'let's walk and count to sixty.'

'But . . .'

'Trust me. One. Two. Three.'

Ella joined in. 'Four. Five. Six . . .'

They didn't get to sixty. At forty-seven
Ella shouted, 'LOOK! My hat! On the
rock up ahead.' She ran to fetch it.

'The cave worm tricked us! We're
walking around in circles!'

'Did you hear that?' Ella asked.

'What?'

They listened. It was a snigger. A
strange worm-like snigger. Ella saw a flick
of the cave worm's tail. The pink light got
brighter.

'CUTHBERT!' Leo yelled. 'We're trying
to return the magical objects to their
rightful owners and you're going to mess
it all up!'

The cave worm slithered into view.

'I AM LOYAL TO THE BUCKLE
CROWN. I WILL NEVER HELP EVIL
GRISELDA'S CLOCKWORK SPIES.'

'We are NOT clockwork spies.' Ella

stuck out her tongue and did a cartwheel to prove the point, but the cave worm just looked confused.

'Look, Cuthbert,' began Leo. 'We are Warm Hearts. And if we don't return the Incredible Crystallator to the High Chief of the Hob Goblins we won't be able to help Izzambard.'

Suddenly, the Incredible Crystallator (that was still hanging around Ella's neck, despite the cartwheel), began to blink and flash. A bright white light darted around the cave.

Cuthbert flinched. 'Why didn't you tell me you had the Incredible Crystallator!'

'We did,' Ella replied.

'But I didn't believe you.' Cuthbert had stopped shouting. 'Only the Incredible Crystallator can beam that sort of light. So . . . you really are Warm Hearts? And you're here to save our Kingdom?'

'YES!' shouted the children.

Cuthbert gulped and wriggled his tail.
'Then, what are you waiting for? Quick.
Follow me! We must return the Incredible
Crystallator to Gripendulum. Hurry.
Quick! Now! Move! Come this way!
There's no time to lose!'

PLATFORM TWELVE

· THE HIGH CHIEF'S COURT ·

Cuthbert wriggled to the end of a long, winding passage, and walloped his tail end against a crystal button. Another cave opened into an even larger one, at the far end of which there was a high ledge of crystal stone. Ella took off the Incredible Crystallator and held it in front of her. Its light beamed across the cave and lit up the ledge.

'WHO DARES TO ENTER THE HIGH CHIEF'S PRIVATE COURT?'

yelled a thin and piercing voice.

'Two young Warm Hearts, sire,' Cuthbert answered.

'And you have led them here, Cave Worm?' A twisted face appeared from above a ledge. But the shadows made it difficult to see clearly.

Cuthbert shivered. 'Yes, my great lord.'

'And how do you know they're not more of the evil Clockmaker's spies? You have already failed me once. I already have a prison full of moles.'

'Indeed. We're in rather a spot of bother,' called a cheery voice. 'Don't mess with a goblin, that's my advice!' It sounded just like the mole they'd seen on the path. Ella shone the Incredible Crystallator into a dark corner behind them. There were bars lodged into the cave, and behind them, a huddled crowd of shivering moles.

'Oh no! Poor little moles,' Ella exclaimed.

'They are not poor. They are spies. They deserve to be locked up,' shrieked Gripendulum. 'As do you!'

'But we are not clockwork spies,' Ella said.

'No. We are Warm Hearts,' Leo said. 'And we've come to return the Incredible Crystallator.'

Ella held the tiny hammer in the air and everyone gasped as its magnificent light flicked around the cave.

Gripendulum edged forwards onto the ledge. The Incredible Crystallator lit him up like a rock star on stage. (Well, a rock star in overalls, with pointy goblin knees.)

'My Incredible Crystallator,' he bellowed. 'Return it to me now!'

'They will,' said the goblins from

the Furnace. They'd just arrived
at the entrance to the cave. 'Prince
Bartholomew told us that you must do
what the Warm Hearts say. They are
here to reopen the mines and save our
Kingdom.'

Gripendulum peered over the ledge
and stared at Ella and Leo. 'But they look
so unimpressive. And look at their knees.
They're so blunt.'

Ella looked at her knees, too.

'That's because they're not goblins,'
answered Anvil, one of the Furnace
goblins. 'You mustn't hold it against
them.'

'What do they want?' Gripendulum
asked.

'We want you to release the mechanical
moles,' Ella replied.

'No!' shrieked Gripendulum. 'They're

Griselda's spies! I will do no such thing!'
He launched himself off the ledge and
into the cave. Ella clutched the Incredible
Crystallator tight.

The moles blinked from behind the
bars and fiddled with their monocles.
Nothing happened. Since they'd been
imprisoned, Griselda seemed to have
deserted them. They were no good to her
behind bars.

'The mechanical moles do not deserve
to be treated like this! No creature should
be locked up!' said Leo. (He was feeling
like electricity again, and hated to see the
moles shiver.) 'Let them free and we will
give you what you want.'

'By Jove, this chap is rather marvellous,'
said one of the moles.

Ella beamed with pride and waved
the Incredible Crystallator. It shone a

beautiful warm light on the imprisoned mechanical moles as they all cheered.

'I will not release them,' shouted Gripendulum. 'Griselda wants to destroy the mines! These are her evil minions.'

'Gosh. Right. Griselda. Destroy the mines? Well, I never . . . May I suggest something, my old chap?' The sergeant of the moles pressed his snout against the bars. 'We moles didn't know Griselda was such a bad egg. Just thought she helped us how to see. But if all you say is true— if she stopped the goblins mining Fairy Dust—well. Terrible business.'

'It's all true, Sergeant Mole,' Ella shouted. 'She's destroying the Kingdom of Izzambard and getting rid of all the Old Magic!'

The shivering moles gasped.

'In that case,' the sergeant bellowed, 'it

113

would be an honour to help the Warm
Hearts. If you release us from this stone
enclosure, we will help you reopen the
mines. Even without Griselda's monocles,
we can still dig all the entrances clear.
Help the goblins. Work together. Get the
whole Fairy Dust thing back on track.'

'We don't want your help,'
Gripendulum sneered. 'You're Griselda's
spies.'

'Not if we take these off.' The sergeant
ripped off his monocle and threw it on the
ground. 'Chaps. Monocles off. We don't
need them anymore. The Clockmaker
is no good and tells lies. She starts Fairy
Wars, closes mines, and destroys Old
Magic. Let's go back to the Old Ways.
Buckle Times. Sniff our way around like
we used to. Warm Hearts and Fairy Dust
are the future!'

The moles all threw their monocles on the floor and cheered.

'Shall I pick up the monocles, sergeant?' asked a tiny mole. 'And pass them through the bars so the goblins can recycle them in the Furnace?'

'Marvellous idea,' the sergeant answered.

Gripendulum leapt down from his ledge and spun around sixteen times. (That's what Hob Goblins do when they need to think.) Then he stopped. A hush whispered through the caves:

'THE HIGH CHIEF HAS DECIDED. IF THE WARM-HEART CHILD GIVES ME THE INCREDIBLE CRYSTALLATOR, I WILL RELEASE THE MECHANICAL MOLES.'

Suddenly, the goblins lifted Ella and Leo in the air and started to cheer. 'Put

me down! Put me down!' Ella wriggled
out of the goblins' hands and ran across
the cave to Gripendulum.

BLINKETTY FLASH BLINKETTY FLASH

Very carefully, she pulled the Incredible
Crystallator from around her neck and
placed the tiny shiny hammer in the High
Chief of the Hob Goblins' hands.

'Ahhhhhh!' Gripendulum sighed and licked his cheeks three times (goblins have very long tongues). 'At last!' he laughed, 'the Incredible Crystallator is back where it belongs.'

BLINKETTY FLASH BLINKETTY FLASH

'I see you have missed me!' Gripendulum curled his tongue back into his mouth and smiled. 'We have missed you, too! And we tried to make other hammers to replace you, but they couldn't even make a dent in the deep seams of Fairy Dust. Only you, the Incredible Crystallator, have the power to break the crystal.'

BLINKETTY FLASH

Ella and Leo smiled. (Returning a hammer to its rightful goblin felt a bit like returning a lost lamb to its mother ewe. Or returning a lost wallet to its owner. You

just know you've done the right thing.)
Gripendulum whispered some strange
gobliny words and breathed his hot goblin
breath upon the hammer. Then, the most
amazing thing happened: the cave lit up
and, as if from nowhere, more than a
hundred sparkling hammers burst from
the Incredible Crystallator and clattered
onto the floor.

Gripendulum leapt into the air with
glee and licked his cheeks once more.
'Oh, Incredible Crystallator. You are the
mother of all tools. Goblins: gather your
hammers. There is work to be done!'

The goblins rushed forwards and
picked up their shining hammers. Then,
they bowed until their chins scraped
the floor, just waiting for instruction.
'Now, dear grovelling goblins,' began
Gripendulum, 'you must find the deepest

and richest Fairy Dust seams . . .'

'WAIT!' shouted Ella.

A goblin murmur rumbled through the cave.

'What is it, red-hatted Warm Heart?' asked Gripendulum.

'What about the moles?'

'Yes. You promised to release them,' said Leo.

'Oh. Absolutely. Hear hear. Spot on,' said the sergeant.

Gripendulum licked his cheeks three times and put one hand in his pocket, pulling out an enormous key. 'Of course, my Warm Hearts. A High Chief always keeps his promise.' In a cave still lit by the light of a hundred hammers, Gripendulum gave the key to Leo. Leo raced across to the dark side of the cave and opened the prison gate. 'No-longer-mechanical moles, you are fr— Oh!'

'What's the matter?' Ella asked.

'The key's snapped in the lock,' Leo said, shaking the prison door.

'Then they are stuck in the prison for ever,' shrieked Gripendulum. 'I will have to think of a cunning goblin plan.' The High Chief Hob Goblin started spinning in the air, as that's what thinking goblins do.

The moles all shivered and sighed.

'Wait,' Ella said. 'If you are moles, then surely you can just dig downwards? You don't need to get out through the door!'

'Blimey. The Warm Heart's got a point! Come on chaps, let's start digging.'

It took them a little while to dig through the hard cave floor, but with Ella and Leo's encouragement, the prison was soon full of nothing but earth, and they all resurfaced in the main cave. The sergeant scampered over to Leo and sniffed his legs. Then, he scurried over to Ella and sniffed hers.

Ella giggled. Mechanical moles were lovely, especially without their mechanical bits.

Gripendulum had been spinning in the air for a considerable length of time, so he was a little bit dizzy when he eventually dropped to the floor and clapped his hands together. 'I have an idea.'

'Emergency over. We're all free.' The sergeant beamed.

Gripendulum frowned. But then he remembered that he was *still* magnificent. He was *still* High Chief of the Hob Goblins. And he *still* had the Incredible Crystallator. He licked his cheeks three times and smiled: 'I declare the Crystal Cave Mines OPEN. PRODUCTION OF FAIRY DUST—**BEGIN!**'

PLATFORM THIRTEEN

· FAREWELLS AND FEATHERS ·

Soon, every corner of the Crystal Caves was alive with light, laughter, and the **CLINK** of hammers. Goblins worked alongside moles, moles worked alongside fairies, and crates of Fairy Dust appeared at the entrance of every cave. (Yes. Even the fairies were helping—flying pots of dust to the creatures that needed it most.) Gripendulum's spirits had lifted, the Fairy Feuds were forgotten, and the cracks and creaks of bridges and mountains had gone.

'Come on, Ella!' Leo said. 'I know you love it here, but we must get back to the train.' Ella was letting some of the smallest moles balance on her hat. 'When Griselda finds out about the moles' mutiny, she'll be furious. And anyway, we mustn't keep the Angerwick waiting.'

'You are right,' Ella replied, putting the moles down gently and shaking their tiny paws.

Ella and Leo said their farewells to Gripendulum, Cuthbert, and the rest of the no-longer-mechanical moles, and with three of the Furnace goblins carrying a crate of Fairy Dust behind them, began their long walk along the crystal path back to the train.

'Wait!' Gripendulum shouted. 'That way will take far too long. Follow me. I will show you to my personal cart.' He led them off the path and into a dark tunnel that led into an unused mine.

'Are you sure this is a good idea?' Leo asked. 'Your cart looks a little bit rusty.'

'Of course—it will be fine.'

Gripendulum licked the orange rust away with his tongue and spat it on the floor.

Ella tried not to say 'YUCK' out loud. She knew that Gripendulum had very good manners. They were just different from Warm Heart ones.

'Hop in!' Gripendulum smiled.

'Don't go without us!' It was Nut Snap and Ice Splatter. Only Nut Snap and Ice Splatter had changed.

'You look different,' Ella exclaimed.

'Oh. We are. We're beautiful again. Aren't we? Utterly gorgeous?'

Leo sniggered as Ice Splatter fluttered her wings. 'We just wanted to say thank you. It's the Fairy Dust, you see. Our hairy chins and heavy wings have gone! The goblins delivered some crates to our tribes and we're all feeling ourselves again. War has been cancelled. Oh yes. We're ever so happy and such best friends. Thank you, dear High Chief

Gripendulum.'

Gripendulum span around thrice.

'And we haven't bitten each other for ages, have we, Nut Snap?!'

'No, Ice Splatter,' said Nut Snap, looking longingly at Ice Splatter's tasty ear.

'That's wonderful news,' Leo said. 'But we really must go. We have a prince to return to and an Angerwick to soothe.'

'Oh yes!' said Ella. 'He might explode!'

The little group of goblins heaved the crate of Fairy Dust into the cart, and before Ella and Leo could say goodbye to the fairies, Gripendulum licked his cheeks three times and pushed hard. With the three goblins, Ella and Leo, and the crate of Fairy Dust squeezed in, the cart whizzed into the darkness at high speed.

And he was right. They turned the

corner and there, at the sparkling, star-grain platform, was a bright plum-coloured engine and a big puff of chuggetty steam.

The Asquiths waved their tails in greeting as the goblins lifted the crate of Fairy Dust onto the train. Barty was waving his cap and beaming, and Cogg was flashing his lights, showing off his new nozzle. 'I knew you'd do it,' shouted Barty. 'You clever, clever Warm Hearts! Come on! Hop on the train. The Angerwick is waiting.'

'Goodbye goblins,' said Ella, kissing their little chins. Leo shook their goblin hands.

'Goodbye, dearest magical Warm Hearts.' The three goblins bowed very, very low.

PLATFORM FOURTEEN

· THE POWER OF FAIRY DUST ·

'THE TRAIN IS NOW ARRIVING AT
THE VALLEY OF THE ANGERWICK.
WE WILL BE STOPPING ON THE
VIADUCT. PLEASE DO NOT GET OFF.
I REPEAT. PLEASE DO NOT GET
OFF.'

'Is it time to wake the Angerwick?' Ella
asked, leaning out of the carriage window.
'We promised to make his creaky knees
better.'

'Of course,' Barty replied. 'I'll leave

130

that to you.'

Barty grabbed a pot of Fairy Dust and so did Leo.

As soon as the train stopped, Ella jumped onto the bridge and stood extremely still. Then she took a deep breath. (There is very little in life that is more exciting than waking an Angerwick. On purpose!) Having breathed in the moment, she grinned and looked around the railway tracks for a pebble.

'Will this one do?' she called. Leo and Barty turned around. Ella was holding up a large lump of diamond-like crystal.

'Perfect. Now throw it down. Try not to hurt him. Try to make it land near his toes.'

'D . . . d . . . don't light his fuse.' Barty sounded just a little bit nervous.

Ella pushed her hat away from her

eyes, took aim and threw the crystal hard. It shone as it spun in the sunlight. Leo and Barty put their pots down and peered over the bridge to watch. The shining stone bounced off the sides of the ravine and into the abyss.

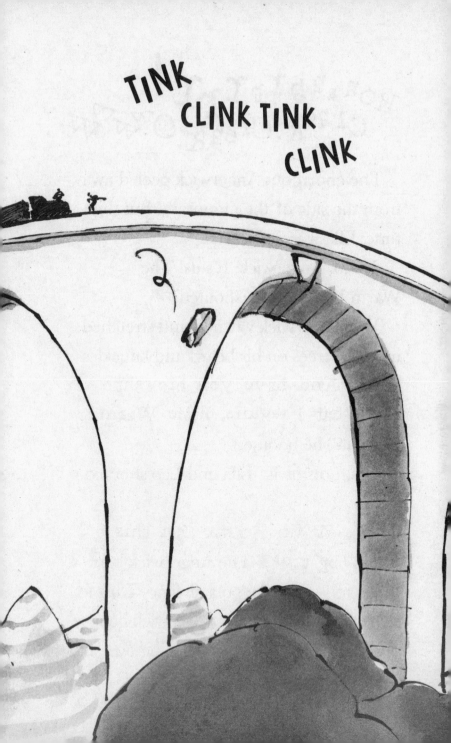

Roaaaarrrrr!
crack.Creak.Owwww.

The enormous Angerwick peeled away
from the side of the mountain. But this
time, Ella was not scared.

'Hello, Angerwick. It's us! The
Warm Hearts,' Ella shouted.

The Angerwick yawned and stretched
until the trees on his beard and knuckles
shook. 'And have you brought
me what I require, little Warm
Hearts?' he boomed.

'Yes, Lots of it,' Ella and Leo shouted
back.

'Oh, Warm Hearts. Can this
really be true?' The Angerwick bent
down to look at the pots of Fairy Dust in
their hands. (When an Angerwick bends
down it's like a mountain folding over, but

Ella and Leo still weren't scared.)

The Angerwick started to laugh. Goblinora bridge trembled and Ella and Leo held onto the sides.

'Oh. But my joints ache so, dear Warm Hearts,' bellowed the Angerwick. cracK. 'Please blow a little Fairy Dust into the air.'

'What? Just a little?' Ella asked.

'Will that be enough for your bones?' Leo wondered how a tiny bit of Fairy Dust could help an Angerwick the size of a mountain.

'Of course.' The Angerwick smiled. 'Fairy Dust is a VERY powerful thing.'

Leo held his pot over the side of the bridge and blew just a handful towards the Angerwick. What happened next is hard to explain. But it was more beautiful

135

than an Other World night sky lit with a thousand shooting stars. They both watched as the enormous, mountainous body of the Angerwick started to shine. His rivers sparkled. His trees turned green. The cracks in his dark granite rocks all disappeared! The Angerwick was transformed. He was . . . well . . . he was . . . WONDERFUL.

The Angerwick breathed in deeply and sighed into the air.

Leo and Ella turned their faces, held their breath, and clutched their noses tight.

The Angerwick laughed. 'Silly Warm Hearts. Now my body is refreshed with Fairy Dust, I am no longer heavy with sleep. My eyes are bright, and my rivers flow clear. You are in no danger.

Fear not. My breath will not
harm you.'

'Oh. Phew.' Ella turned her face back
to the Angerwick.

'In fact, dear Warm Hearts,
as you have cured my pains,
I would like to swear an
Angerwick Oath. By all that
is Mighty and Fair, I give the
Angerwick Word that I will use
my strength to defend Old Magic
against its enemies and help all
Warm Hearts through time.'

'Wow, thanks!' (Leo knew that 'Wow,
thanks!' was a rubbish thing to say. He
should have said something grand like:
'We Warm Hearts accept with gratitude.'
But that's not how life works. You only
think of the right things to say when it's
all over and no one is listening.)

138

'If ever you require my help,' boomed the Angerwick, 'just throw a crystal into my abyss.'

'I LOVE Angerwicks,' shouted Ella. Leo smiled. That was a much better thing to say.

Lord and Lady Asquith pulled some levers.

'All aboard,' Barty shouted, jumping on the train. Cogg, Leo, and Ella followed.

HISSS KERSPLUTTER HSSSS
CHOOOOOOO
CHOOOOOOOOoooooo

The train started to move.

CHUG CHUG CHUGGETY
CHUG

PLATFORM FIFTEEN

· HOME TIME AND PUDDING ·

Ella didn't want to go back to the Other
World.

'Now, now.' Barty dabbed Ella's
tears away with his hankie. 'Don't be
sad. If adventures didn't come to an
end, new ones could never begin. And
remember: whenever you want to come
to Izzambard, Cogg and I will always be
waiting.'

'But what about Griselda?' Ella sniffed.
'She might hurt you and destroy all the
Old Magic.'

'Not now you have opened the mines and filled our Kingdom with Fairy Dust again. There is still work to be done and curses to break, but Griselda is losing her power. And it's all thanks to you two.'

'I still don't want to go home!' Ella grabbed Cogg's nozzle.

'What if Griselda starts to play about with time?' Leo said. 'You don't want Mum and Dad to miss us.'

Cogg vacuumed Ella on the back.

'Anyway,' Barty continued, 'when you are back in the Other World, you might be able to find another of the magical objects. Something that will help us to get past the heronites and the clockwork guards at the Clockmaker's Palace and stop Griselda once and for all. Wouldn't that be wonderful?'

Ella nodded and tried to be brave.

CHOOOOOOO CHOOOOOOOO!

The train was coming into the station. Platform One. The Other World. Barty didn't announce the station. Not this time. He was a bit too full of tears!

Leo patted Barty on the shoulder and shook his hand. 'Keep the Kingdom safe while we're gone.'

'I will.' Barty tried to smile.

'We'll come back soon. Promise.' Ella flung herself around Barty one last time, then jumped onto the platform with Leo.

They both waved at the twitching

Asquiths as the gleaming plum-coloured train chugged away.

Griselda's mechanical vines started to creak ominously. 'Quick, Leo. Open the door. Oh. No. It's the one without a handle.'

CREEEEAAK

Leo had forgotten all about the Sleeping Key. He rummaged around in his pockets. **PHEW!** It was still there. He took it out and held it towards the door.

SNIFF

The Sleeping Key sniffed its way towards the lock

and the door sprang open. The children pushed their way through.

'Yuck! It's dusty. But it's not like twinkly Fairy Dust,' Ella said.

'Of course it's not.' Leo ran through the clutter of the workshop and into the fresh air. 'Shall we look for another magical object now?' Ella started to climb on the boxes.

'No,' Leo said, dashing back and taking her hand. 'Now we're back in the Other World, time will start to move here again, and Mum and Dad will miss us. Come on, Ella. Race you. Let's go home.'

Ella didn't need persuading. Now they were in the Other World things felt different, and as soon as Leo said the words 'Mum and Dad', Ella started missing them, too.

* * *

'MUM,' Leo shouted as he and his sister ran back into the station house. 'We're back!'

'Perfect timing,' said Mrs Leggit, hardly bothering to turn around,

'Didn't you miss us?' asked Ella.

'Why would I? You've only been gone a minute, you dafties. Now, can you go and help your father? He wants to put some pictures up. But he says he's lost his hammer. Which is strange. I thought he had it a minute ago. Perhaps there's one at the workshop?'

'There was,' Ella said.

'But there isn't anymore,' Leo said.

'Pardon?' Mrs Leggit replied.

'Well, we have seen one,' Ella explained. 'A magical one called the Incredible Crystallator. But we had to give it back.'

'Give it back to whom?' asked Mrs Leggit.

'Gripendulum—the High Chief of the Hob Goblins,' Ella said.

'Oh, not that again,' sighed Mrs Leggit. 'Look. Just take this shoe to your father.' She handed Leo a boot with a very firm heel. 'Tell him he'll have to use that. And when you've finished helping him, go and have a wash. You both look a little bit dusty!'

'It's probably Fairy Dust,' Ella explained.

Leo nodded.

'Fairy Dust! Whatever next? You children have such wonderful

imaginations! Now go and freshen up and
we'll make some sticky toffee pudding.
With a bit of cream. Just the way you
like.'

'Brilliant!' Leo smiled. Ella smiled,
too. She was going to miss Izzambard
terribly. And she couldn't wait to go on

Cat Among
the Pigeons

JULIA GOLDING

CAT GOES TO SCHOOL

EGMONT

For Grace, Robert, Olivia and
Miranda Amakye Saunders

EGMONT

We bring stories to life

First published 2006
by Egmont UK Ltd
The Yellow Building, 1 Nicholas Road, London W11 4AN
This edition published 2010

Text copyright © 2006 Julia Golding

The moral rights of the author have been asserted

Bowles's New Plan of London map courtesy of the British Library

ISBN 978 1 4052 3759 8

A CIP catalogue record for this title is available from the British Library

Printed and bound in the UK by CPI Group (UK) Ltd, Croydon, CR0 4YY

44217/9

www.egmont.co.uk
www.juliagolding.co.uk